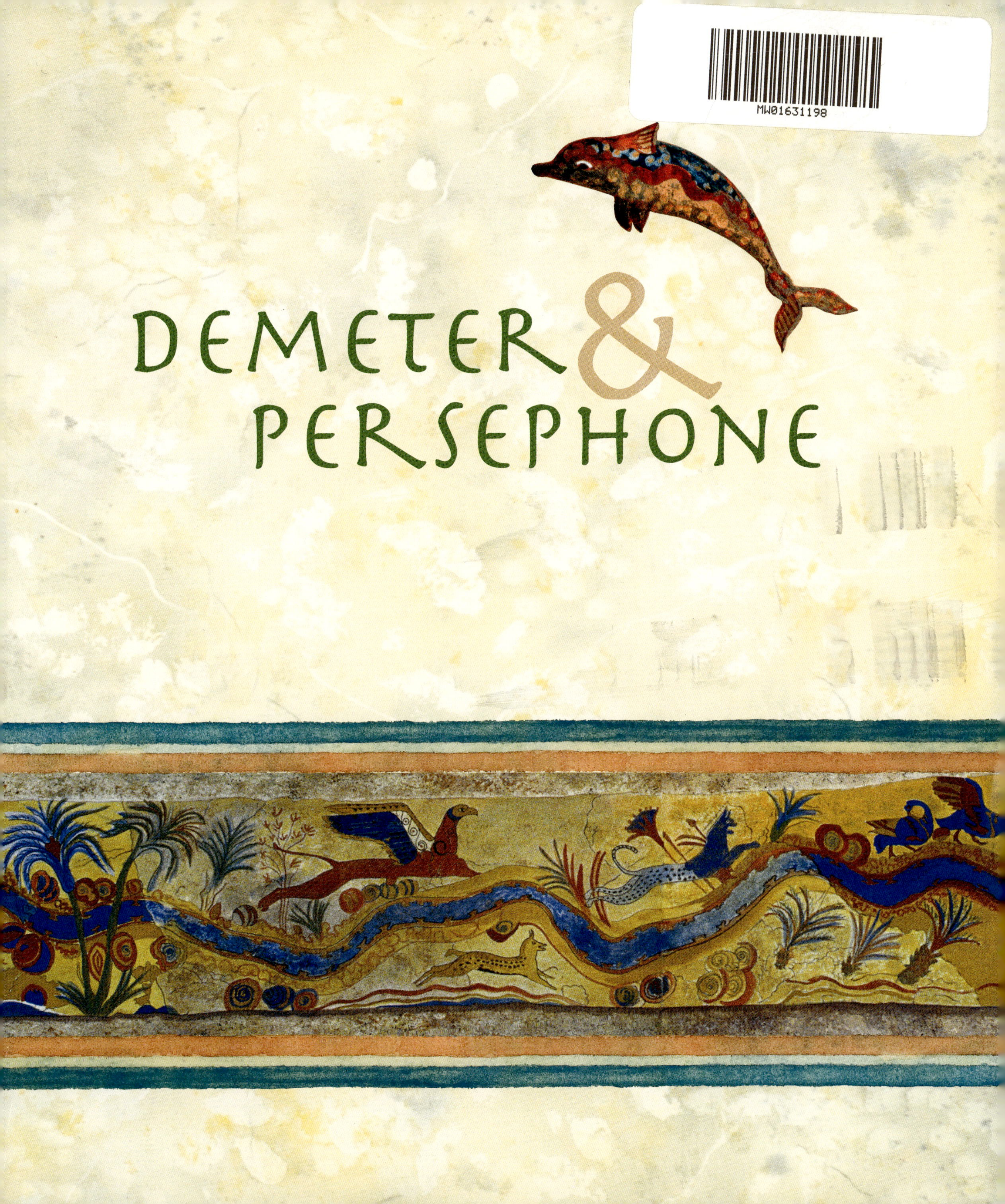

MW01631198
DEMETER & PERSEPHONE

Adapted & illustrated by

Marjorie Meyers Graham

www.marjoriegraham.com

A production of

A Woman's Place
Retreats and Seminars
Celebrating Women and
Creativity since 1995

Book design by Ingrid Hess

ISBN:978-1-4243-2244-2

Printed in China

THE ARCHETYPAL MYTH OF

DEMETER & PERSEPHONE

A STORY FOR MOTHER & DAUGHTER CELEBRATIONS

MARJORIE MEYERS GRAHAM

DEDICATED TO
MY MOTHER, DAUGHTERS &
GRANDDAUGHTERS

IN LOVING MEMORY OF
MY THREE GRANDMOTHERS

WITH GRATEFUL THANKS TO
MY HUSBAND & MANY SISTERS

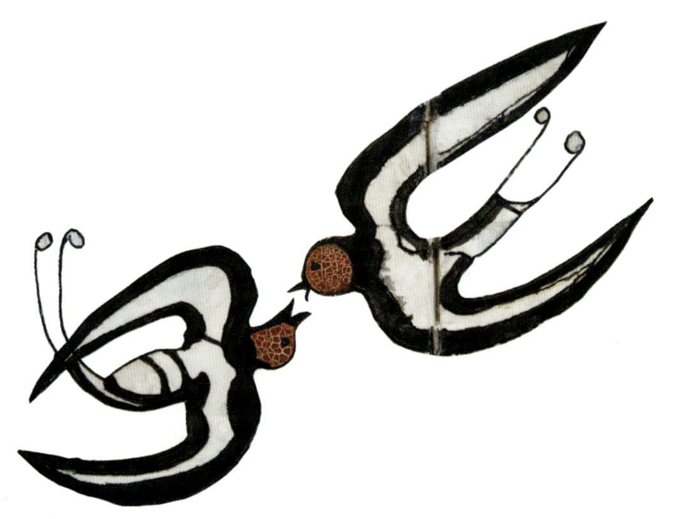

TABLE OF CONTENTS

MYTHOS

INTRODUCTION TO DEMETER & PERSEPHONE

For thousands of years before the beginning of Judaism, Christianity, or Islam, girls and their mothers celebrated the changing seasons together in special, sacred rituals. Mother Nature was honored for her gift of all life, and special ceremonies marked the changing cycle of each year.

This is the story of springtime as scholars think it was told before the invention of writing in Greece, before men became more powerful than women. Ancient myths are stories which explained the mysteries of life and nature and helped human beings live together. The death of nature in autumn and winter, followed by the rebirth of nature in springtime was considered a sacred mystery; this story was recited and acted out by women around March 20, known to us as the spring, or vernal, equinox.

"The Gift of Myth" The Goddess presents the famous Phaistos Disc, which is still untranslated (ca. 1700–1600 B.C.E, Heraklion Archeological Museum, Crete)

My purpose in creating this book is to share with girls and their moms one of my favorite stories, an ancient tale that still feels new, that can help us understand our own relationships with our mothers and daughters. This story, or myth, touches something in all females, for we are all daughters of our mothers, and we all eventually need to leave our moms and go out on our own into the world to make our own places, to develop our gifts, to "do our own thing." Yet the strong, loving bond between mothers and daughters can grow even deeper as a result.

I also hope to share with women of all ages a taste of the time before patriarchy, when the central deities were female, when families were still organized around the maternal figure and when the wisdom of women was cherished by everyone. The Women's Sacred Circle on the next page shows the eight dates of the ancient seasonal rituals, which women celebrated by acting out myths such as this one. What follows is the ancient story of Demeter and Persephone scripted for three readers so you will be able to experience it that way.

So, when you are riding your bike or just playing outside and you notice all the little buds are suddenly popping out on bushes, and when you see crocuses and daffodils in the beautiful warm springtime, think of the magic ring of purple crocuses around Demeter, whispering *"Persephone returns!"* And picture all of nature rejoicing and celebrating in the happiness of the mother and daughter reunion.

MARJORIE M. GRAHAM

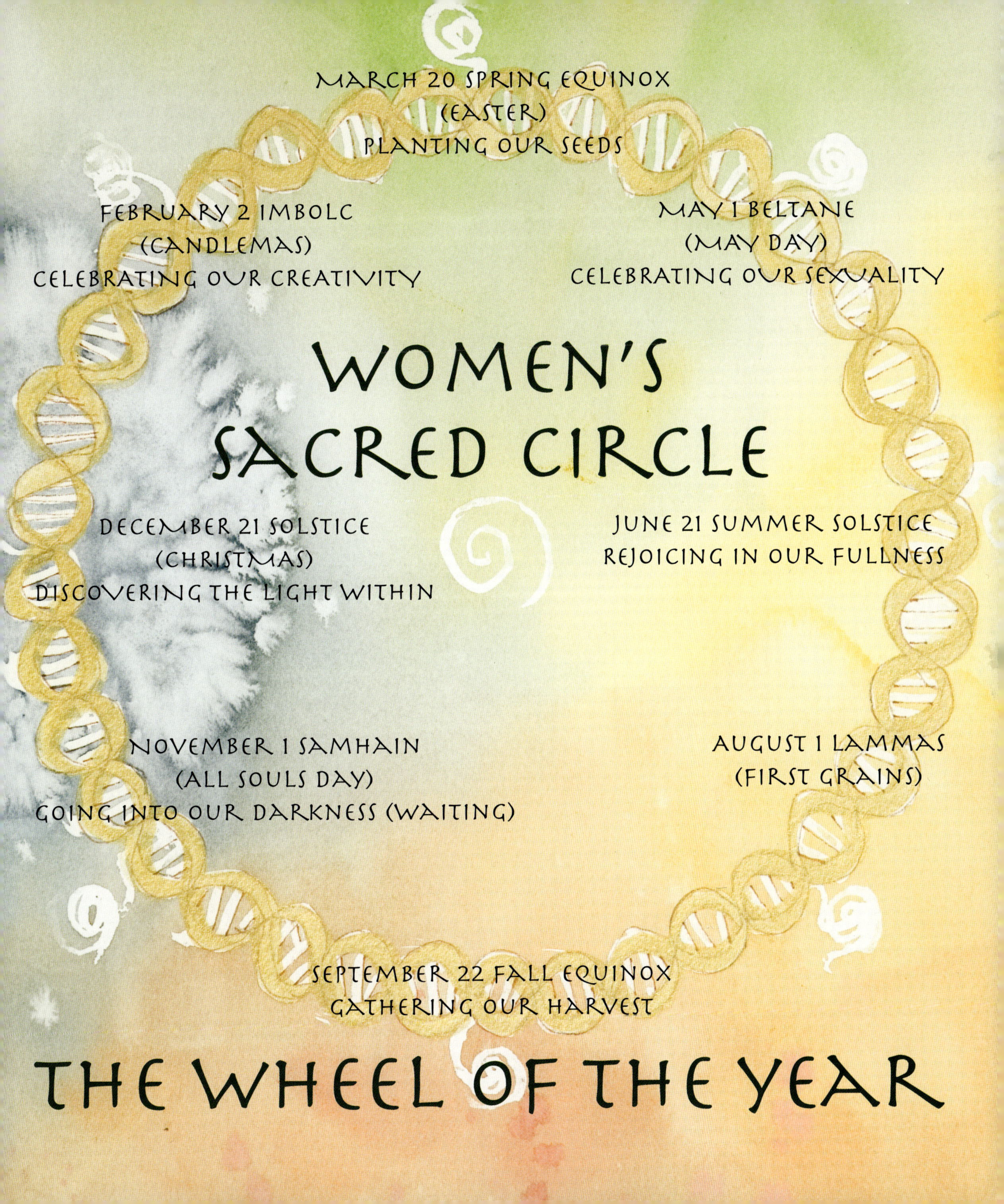

March 20 Spring Equinox
(Easter)
Planting Our Seeds

February 2 Imbolc
(Candlemas)
Celebrating Our Creativity

May 1 Beltane
(May Day)
Celebrating Our Sexuality

Women's Sacred Circle

December 21 Solstice
(Christmas)
Discovering the Light Within

June 21 Summer Solstice
Rejoicing in Our Fullness

November 1 Samhain
(All Souls Day)
Going into Our Darkness (Waiting)

August 1 Lammas
(First Grains)

September 22 Fall Equinox
Gathering Our Harvest

The Wheel of the Year

Act 1:
Eternal Summer

Storyteller:

Once upon a time there was no winter. Leaves and vines, flowers and grass grew into fullness and faded into decay, then began again in unceasing rhythms.

Men joined with other men of their mother's clan and foraged in the evergreen woods for game. Women, with their children or grandchildren toddling behind them, explored the thick growth of plants encircling their homes. Over time, they learned which ones bore fruits that satisfied hunger, which bore leaves and roots that chased illness and pain, and which worked magic on the eye, mouth and head.

DEMETRA GIVES MORTALS THE GIFT OF WHEAT AND AGRICULTURE
δίνει στους θνητούς ως δώρο το σιτάρι και τη

The mother goddess Demeter watched fondly as the mortals learned more and more about her plants. Seeing that their lives were difficult and their food supply sporadic, she was moved to give them the gift of wheat. She showed them how to plant the seed, cultivate, and finally harvest the wheat and grind it. The mortals always entrusted the essential process of planting food to the women, in the hope that their fertility of womb might be transferred to the fields they touched.

THE GODDESS DEMETER

EARLY DEMETER The mother goddess Demeter was associated with fertility goddesses from other prehistoric cultures, such as the Egyptian goddess Isis. Demeter was probably introduced into Greece from Minoan Crete. The second part of *Demeter* means "mother."

THE TWO GODDESSES Demeter was closely associated with her daughter, Persephone, often pictured together as "Mother and Daughter" and also known as "The Two Goddesses." Another early name for the daughter was "Kore".

HER CULT Credited with giving humans the knowledge of growing grain, Demeter was also associated with fertility, motherly nurturing and the cycle of the seasons. Demeter and her daughter were rustic goddesses, worshipped outdoors and often at harvest time. They developed a faithful following, or cult, that practiced important annual ceremonies of initiation known as mysteries at Eleusis, near Athens, for many centuries. The fertility-based Eleusinian Mysteries were continued even into Roman and Christian times (see p. 14).

HER ANCESTRY Influenced by the writings of Homer and Hesiod, people in the Classical Greek period believed that Demeter was the daughter of two of the Titans, Kronos and Rhea, who were children of Gaia, the Great Earth Mother Goddess.

The mother goddess Demeter had a fair-born daughter, Persephone, who watched over the crops with her Mother. Persephone was drawn especially to the new sprouts of wheat that pushed their way through the soil in her favorite shade of tender green. She loved to walk among the young plants, beckoning them upward and stroking the weaker shoots.

GRAIN AGRICULTURE AND CIVILIZATION

For many thousands of years, human beings hunted and gathered food to survive. To do this, they had to move from one place to the next, following the herds of wild animals and searching for new sources of food. The women and children gathered and prepared fruits, nuts, roots and berries to eat, furnishing their group with much of its nutrition. When humans understood that seeds contain the power to grow wheat and corn, they were able to settle down and build dwellings and create what we call civilization.

AGRICULTURE Knowing how to plant seeds and grow grain gave prehistoric people the ability to produce their own food, beginning around 10,000 years ago. They no longer had to wander to find food, but could stay put in a chosen spot and farm the land. Soon the bronze plow was invented, greatly increasing the amount of land that could be farmed.

CIVILIZATION Being able to settle in one place gave humans the leisure to develop skills in weaving, pottery, architecture, and metallurgy. Various goods could then be traded between neighboring settled communities, or carried in ships to far-off places.

SEEDS A kernel of wheat or corn can be planted in the earth, and with moisture and warm sunshine, it will sprout and grow into a tall stalk which can be harvested to produce more nutritious food as well as hundreds of new, fertile seeds. Many heads of wheat and corn will grow from one single seed.

DEMETER'S GIFT Grain agriculture was considered a mysterious gift to mankind from the goddess Demeter; she was often pictured holding sheaves of wheat. The Eleusinian mystery cult practiced secret initiation rituals for approximately 2,000 years in honor of Demeter (see p. 14).

Persephone loves the new sprouts
αγαπαι τα βλαστάρια

Later, when the plants approached maturity, Persephone would leave their care to her Mother and wander over the hills, gathering narcissus, hyacinth, and garlands of myrtle for Demeter's hair. Persephone herself favored the bold red poppies that sprang up among the wheat.

It was not unusual to see Demeter and Persephone decked with flowers, dancing together through open fields and gently sloping valleys. When Demeter felt especially fine, tiny shoots of barley or oats would spring up in her footprints.

WHAT ARE MYTHS AND ARCHETYPES?

MYTHS Myths are powerful, ancient stories of events and relationships that explain aspects of the natural world or of a society's origins.

"A myth is a depersonalized dream," said visionary mythologist Joseph Campbell. Spirituality scholar Jean Houston believes that "a myth is something that never was but is always happening." (as quoted in Elizabeth Davis and Carol Leonard, *The Women's Wheel of Life*, p. 3)

ARCHETYPES Certain characters in mythology, such as the mother and daughter goddesses Demeter and Persephone, express eternal aspects of human nature. Such figures are called archetypes, which some psychologists believe have been alive in the human imagination since the beginning of our species, patterns of thought or imagery inherited from past collective experience.

Psychologist Jean Bolen defines them as "powerful inner patterns . . . [and] dominant forces within us," strongly linked to myth. "The purpose of familiarizing ourselves with archetypes is to better understand our behavior, our responses to certain situations in life, our deepest longings and desires" (Davis and Leonard, p. 3).

DEMETRA
Η Δήμητρα
PERSEPHON
Η Περσεφον

ACT II:
AUTUMN

STORYTELLER:
One day, they were sitting on the slope of a high hill, looking out in many directions over Demeter's fields of grain. Persephone lay on her back while her Mother idly stroked her long hair.

PERSEPHONE:
Mother, sometimes in my wanderings, I have met the spirits of the dead hovering around their earthly homes, and sometimes the mortals, too, can see them in the dark of the moon by the light of their fires and torches.

DEMETER:
Those are spirits who drift about restlessly, but they mean no harm.

PERSEPHONE:
I spoke to them, Mother. They seem confused and many do not even understand their own state. Is there no one in the underworld who receives the new dead?

DEMETER:

It is I who have domain over the underworld. From beneath the surface of the earth I draw forth the crops and the wild plants. I have instructed the mortals to store seed from their harvests in pits beneath the earth. This contact with the spirits of my underworld will fertilize the seed for sowing the next crop. Yes, I know very well the realm of the dead, but my most important work is here. I must feed the living.

STORYTELLER:

Persephone rolled over and thought about the ghostly spirits she had seen, about their faces drawn with pain and bewilderment, and she said,

PERSEPHONE:

The dead need us, Mother. I will go to them.

STORYTELLER:

Demeter abruptly sat upright as a chill passed through her and rustled the grass around them. She was speechless for a moment, but then hurriedly began recounting all the pleasures they enjoyed in their world of sunshine, warmth, and fragrant flowers. She told her daughter of the dark gloom of the underworld and begged her to reconsider.

Persephone sat up and hugged her Mother and rocked her with silent tears. For a long while they held each other radiating rainbow auras of love and protection.
Yet Persephone's response was unchanged.

They stood and walked in silence down the slope toward the fields. Finally they stopped, surrounded by Demeter's grain, and shared weary smiles.

THE ELEUSINIAN MYSTERY CULT

Homer's "Hymn to Demeter" informs us that Demeter came from Crete but established the mysteries at Eleusis.

From approximately 1450 B.C. until well into the Roman era, the Goddess Demeter was worshipped and her mysteries were revealed to initiates in the temple complex at Eleusis, near the sea about 15 miles west of Athens, Greece (see map, p. 36). Today the area is a large archeological site surrounded by the industrial city called "Elefsina."

ELEUSIS Developed and expanded over many centuries, the sacred complex at Eleusis contained an enormous court, processional avenues, priests' and priestesses' quarters and temples, as well as the symbolic entrance to the underworld.

THE CULT The worship of Demeter differed from other religious cults of the ancient world in that the faithful were chosen and then underwent elaborate instruction and preparation before they could be initiated. They had to swear to keep secret whatever they learned. As a result, all that we know today is based on ancient hearsay and descriptions of those rituals of the festival that were performed in public.

THE MYSTERIES Celebrated in two parts each year, the Lesser Mysteries were the first stage of the initiation and were held in March, at the spring, or vernal, equinox. Candidates who were properly prepared would then be able to participate in the nine day-long Greater Mysteries at the autumnal equinox in September. Processions, purifications, drama and ritual sacrifices led up to the culminating ecstatic experience after which rites and libations for the dead took place. Finally, religious intitiates "returned to their homes nobler in spirit, contented, less fearful of death and with raised hopes of a better life." (Kalliope Preka-Alexandri, *Eleusis,* p.21)

DEMETER:

Very well, Persephone. You are loving and giving and we cannot give only to ourselves. I understand why you must go. Still, you are my daughter and for every day that you remain in the underworld, I will mourn your absence.

STORYTELLER:

Persephone gathered three poppies and three sheaves of wheat. Then Demeter led her to a long, deep chasm and produced a torch for her to carry. She stood and watched her daughter go down farther and farther into the cleft in the earth.

In the crook of her arm, Persephone held her mother's grain close to her breast, while her other arm held the torch aloft. She was startled by the chill as she descended, but she was not afraid. Deeper and deeper into the darkness she continued, picking her way slowly along the rocky path.

For many hours she was surrounded only by silence. Gradually she became aware of a low moaning sound. It grew in intensity until she rounded a corner and entered an enormous cavern, where thousands of spirits of the dead milled about aimlessly, hugging themselves, shaking their heads, and moaning in despair.

Persephone moved through the forms and climbed up onto a large, flat rock. Then she set up a stand for her torch, a vase for Demeter's grain, and a large shallow bowl piled with pomegranate seeds, the food of the dead. As she stood before them, her aura increased in brightness and in warmth.

PERSEPHONE:
I am Persephone and I have come to be your queen. Each of you has left your earthly body and now resides in the realm of the dead. If you come to me, I will initiate you into your new world.

STORYTELLER:
She beckoned those nearest to step up onto the rock and enter her aura. As each spirit crossed before her, Persephone embraced the form and then stepped back and gazed into its eyes. She then reached for a few of the pomegranate seeds, squeezing them between her fingers. She painted the spirit's forehead with a broad stripe of the red juice and slowly said:

PERSEPHONE:
You have waxed into the fullness of life
And waned into darkness;
May you be renewed in tranquility and wisdom.

STORYTELLER:
And the souls of the dead mortals were comforted and became peaceful in the underworld.

WHO WERE THE MINOANS?

From approximately 3000 to 1000 B.C., during the Bronze Age, the first European civilization developed and flourished on the island of Crete, at the crossroads of Asia, North Africa and Europe. Today, Crete is part of Greece (see map on p. 36).

Called "Minoan" after the perhaps mythical leader King Minos, this relatively peaceful and prosperous prehistoric culture joyfully celebrated life and nature's bounty, which they considered a gift from the Great Earth Mother Goddess, whom they called Potnia.

ACT III:
WINTER

STORYTELLER:

For months, Persephone received and renewed the dead without ever resting or even growing weary. All the while, her Mother remained disconsolate. Demeter roamed the earth, hoping to find her daughter emerging from one of the secret clefts.

In her sorrow, she withdrew her power from the crops, the trees, the plants. She forbade any new growth to blanket the earth. The mortals planted their seed, but the fields remained barren. It was the first winter.

Demeter was consumed with loneliness and finally settled on a bare hillside to gaze out at nothing from sunken eyes. For days and nights, weeks and months, she sat waiting and grieving.

SOME FACTS ABOUT MINOAN CIVILIZATION

TRADE Essentially self-supporting, the Minoans were great merchants and traders, with many fine goods for export, such as olive oil, and fine pottery decorated with sea life, birds and flowers.

SEA TRAVEL Expert sailors, the Minoans were possibly the first naval power in history. They established outposts on many other islands and defended commerce against Mediterranean sea pirates.

PEACE Minoan towns and settlements were often near seaports rather than defensively positioned on inaccessible hilltops or mountains. They had arms and armor and their towns were sometimes fortified, but the emphasis of this culture was on prosperity, peaceful trade and goddess-worship.

ARCHITECTURE The Minoans built huge, maze-like "palaces"—urban complexes containing workshops, storehouses, and commercial, religious and social spaces for thousands of residents. These palaces had sophisticated systems for air flow and indoor plumbing. The most famous example is at Knossos, near Heraklion, on Crete (see map, p. 36).

ART In many ways surprisingly modern, the Minoans produced art of richly decorated pottery and many palace wall paintings of elaborate beauty (see pp. 28–29).

FOOD The Minoans grew wheat, olives and fruit on plains and terraced hillsides. They fished and raised sheep, goats and pigs.

FASHION Elite Minoan men and women wore elegant, sensual clothing made of wool and possibly silk, as well as exquisitely crafted gold jewelry.

ACT IV:
SPRING

STORYTELLER:

One morning, a ring of purple crocus quietly pushed its way through the soil and surrounded Demeter. She looked with surprise at the new arrivals from below and thought what a shame it was that she was too weakened to feel rage at the crocuses for disobeying her order. Then she leaned forward and heard them whisper in the warm breeze.

PURPLE CROCUSES (EVERYONE):

Persephone returns!
Persephone returns!

Demeter leapt to Her feet and ran down the hill, through the fields and into the forests. She waved Her arms and cried,

DEMETER:

Persephone returns!

persephone
περσεφονη
returns
persephone
περσεφονη
Persephone
περσεφονη
περσεφονη
Persephone
Returns

STORYTELLER:

Everywhere her energy was stirring, pushing, bursting forth into tender greenery and pale young petals. Animals shed their old fur and rolled in the fresh, clean grass while birds sang out.

BIRDS (EVERYONE):

Persephone returns!
Persephone returns!

STORYTELLER:

When Persephone ascended from a dark chasm, there was Demeter, waiting with a cape of white crocus for her daughter. They ran to each other and hugged and cried and laughed and hugged and danced and danced and danced.

The mortals saw everywhere the miracles of Demeter's bliss and rejoiced in the new life of spring.

Each winter, they join Demeter in waiting through the bleak season of her daughter's absence.

Each spring, they are renewed by the signs of Persephone's return.

THE END

SOME FACTS ABOUT MINOAN WALL PAINTINGS (FRESCOES)

Early Minoan houses had red plaster walls. Later, after about 1700 B.C., the walls of the palaces and villas were decorated with colorful frescoes. Much of what today's scholars now know about Minoan culture has come from interpreting these brightly colored images of nature, everyday life and sacred ceremonies. Feminine imagery dominated, with graceful and powerful goddess-priestesses and their symbols of birds, animals and flowers.

FRESCO When color or pigment is applied to wet plaster, it bonds chemically with the plaster as the mixture dries. These paintings, known as frescoes, can endure intact for hundreds or even thousands of years.

PALETTE OF COLORS
The Minoans used mineral-derived hues of cerulean and cobalt blues, iron oxide red, yellow ochre, black and white. Minoan artists usually applied these basic colors in clear, bold areas rather than mixing and blending them together.

STYLE Minoan art, especially wall paintings and ceramic decoration, is exquisitely naturalistic yet formalistic in style.

TECHNIQUE The artist etched the design for the wall fresco onto the wet plaster with a blunt point or pressed a piece of string onto the surface to create a guiding outline. Fresco painting is a rapid process which requires a quick and sure hand.

SUBJECT MATTER
Minoan frescoes and pottery featured graceful images of flowers, sea life, birds and animals, mountains, rivers, trees, and human figures in profile. These images were often bordered with stripes and spirals.

ORIGINS The origins of fresco painting are not known, but it was used as early as the Minoan civilization. The way humans were portrayed appears to have been influenced by the Egyptians.

DISCOVERIES Most Minoan frescoes have been found on Crete, in the palaces of Knossos, Agia Triada and Mallia, and also on the nearby island of Thera (Santorini) in the buildings of Akrotiri (see map, p. 36).

MUSEUMS Some original Minoan frescoes can be seen today in the archeological museums in Athens, Heraklion, and Santorini (see opposite).

This Minoan fresco (ca. 1759 B.C.) called "Crocus-Gatherers" was found in the archeological dig at Akrotiri on Thera (Santorini). The different interpretations in this book were inspired by this ancient image.

Demeter & Persephone

Demeter is the Grain-Mother, the giver of crops. Her origins are Cretan, and she has been strongly connected to Gaia[1] and to Isis[2]. Demeter's daughter, Persephone, or Kore, is the Grain-Maiden, who embodies the new crop. Every autumn the women of early Greece observed a three-day, agricultural fertility ritual, the Thesmophoria, in honor of Demeter. The three days were called the Kathodos and Anodos (Down-going and Uprising,) the Nesteia (Fasting), and the Kalligeneia (Fair-Born or Fair Birth).[3] The Thesmophoria, the Arrephoria, the Skirophoria, the Stenia, and the Haloa were rites practiced by women only and were of extremely early origin. They were preserved "in pristine purity down to the late days and were left almost uncontaminated by Olympian usage"; they emerged later in the most widely influential of all Greek rituals, the Eleusinian Mysteries.[4] Isocrates wrote that Demeter brought to Attica "twofold gifts": crops and the rite of initiation; "those who partake of the rite have fairer hopes concerning the end of life."[5]

The Homeric "Hymn to Demeter," assigned to the seventh century B.C., is a story written to explain the Eleusinian Mysteries, which honored Demeter.[6] The tale became famous as "The Rape of Persephone," who was carried off to the underworld and forced to become the bride of Hades. However, prior to the Olympian version of the myth at a rather late date, there was no mention of rape in the ancient cult of Demeter and her daughter, nor was there any rape in the two traditions antecedent to Demeter's mythology.

Archaeology has supported[7] what Diodorus wrote concerning the flow of Egyptian culture into Greece via Crete: "the whole mythology of Hades" was brought from Egypt into Greece and the mysteries of Isis are just like those of Demeter, "the names only being changed."[8] Isis was Queen of the Underworld, sister of Osiris, and passed freely to and from the netherworld. Demeter's other antecedent was Gaia,[9] the ancient Earth-Mother who had power over the underworld because the earth is the abode of the dead.[10] At certain sites in Greece, Demeter was worshipped as "Demeter Chthonia,"[11] and in Athens the dead were called Demetreioi, "Demeter's People"; not only did she bring all things to life, but when they died, she received them back into her bosom.[12] That the maiden form (Kore) of the Goddess would share the functions of the mature form (Demeter), as giver of crops on the earth and ruler of the underworld, is a natural extension. The early Greeks often conceived of their Goddesses in maiden and mature form simultaneously; later the maiden was called "daughter."[13]

In addition to the connections with Isis and Gaia, another theory holds that Persephone (also called Phesephatta) was a very old Goddess of the underworld indigenous to Attica, who was assimilated by the first wave of invaders from the north; the myth of the abduction is believed to be an artificial link that merged Persephone with Demeter's daughter, Kore.[14] Whatever the impulse behind portraying Persephone as a rape victim, evidence indicates that this twist to the story was added after the societal shift from matrifocal to patriarchal, and that it was not part of the original mythology. In fact it is likely that the story of the rape of the Goddess is a historical reference to the invasion of the northern Zeus-worshippers, just as is the story of the stormy marriage of Hera, the native queen who will not yield to the conqueror Zeus.

Although the exact delineation of the pre-Olympian version of the myth of Demeter and Persephone has been lost, the preceding version seeks to approximate the original by employing the surviving clues and evidence.

This extremely ancient and widely revered sacred story of mother and daughter long pre-dates the Judeo-Christian deification of father and son.

CHARLENE SPRETNAK

Lost Goddesses of Early Greece: A Collection of Pre-Hellenic Myths
(Beacon Press, 1992).

ENDNOTES

1. Lewis R. Farnell, *The Cults of the Greek States,* Vol. 3 (Oxford: Oxford University Press, 1907), pp. 28 and 48–50.
2. Jane Ellen Harrison, *The Religion of Ancient Greece* (London: Archibald Constable & Co., Ltd., 1905), pp. 51–52.
3. Harrison, *Prolegomena to the Study of Greek Religion,* pp. 120–131; also R. F. Willetts, *Cretan Cults and Festivals,* (London: Routledge and Kegan Paul), 1962, p.152.
4. Ibid, Harrison. p. 120.
5. Harrison, *The Religion of Ancient Greece,* p. 51.
6. E. O. James, *The Cult of the Mother Goddess: An Archaeological and Documentary Study* (New York: Frederick A. Praeger, Inc., 1959), p. 153.
7. Sir Arthur Evans, *The Earlier Religion of Greece in the Light of Cretan Discoveries* (London: Macmillan and Co., Ltd., 1931), p. 8.
8. Harrison, *The Religion of Ancient Greece,* p. 52.
9. Farnell, pp. 28 and 48–50.
10. Ibid. p. 8.
11. Ibid. pp. 48–50.
12. Harrison, *Myths of Greece and Rome,* p. 73.
13. Harrison, *Prolegomena to the Study of Greek Religion,* pp. 263 and 274.
14. Gunther Zuntz, *Persephone: Three Essays on Religion and Thought in Magna Graecia* (Oxford: Oxford University Press, 1971), pp. 75–77.

ABOUT CHARLENE SPRETNAK

A graduate of St. Louis University, Charlene Spretnak also holds an M.A. in English and American literature from the University of California at Berkeley. Her work is internationally recognized in the areas of spirituality, cultural history, feminist and other social criticism, and ecological thought (green politics, ecofeminism, ecophilosophy). She is one of the founding mothers of the women's spirituality movement; in 1989 she was inducted into the Ohio Hall of Fame in recognition of her writings on spirituality and social justice. She is currently a professor in the Women's Spirituality branch of the Philosophy and Religion Department at the California Institute of Integral Studies, a graduate institute in San Francisco.

SOURCES FOR FURTHER READING

- Baker, Christina Looper and Christina Baker Kline, *The Conversation Begins: Mothers and Daughters Talk About Living Feminism,* Bantam, 1996.
- Balistier, Thomas, *The Phaistos Disk: An Accounting of Its Unsolved Mystery,* Mahringen, 2000.
- Baring, Ann and Jules Cashford, *The Myth of the Goddess: Evolution of an Image,* Arkana, 1993.
- Bolen, Jean Shinoda, *Goddesses in Everywoman: A New Psychology of Women,* Harper, 1984.
- Cahill, Susan, *Mothers: Memories, Dreams and Reflections by Literary Daughters,* Meridian, 1988.
- Carlson, Kathie, *Life's Daughter/Death's Bride: Inner Transformations Through the Goddess Demeter/Persephone,* Shambhala, 1997.
- Castleden, Rodney, *Minoans: Life in Bronze Age Crete,* Routledge, 1990.
- Davaras, Costis, *Guide to Cretan Antiquities,* Noyes Press, 1976.
- Davis, Elizabeth and Carol Leonard, *The Women's Wheel of Life: Thirteen Archetypes of Woman at Her Fullest Power,* Penguin/Arkana, 1996.
- Debold, Elizabeth, Marie Wilson and Idelisse Malave, *Mother Daughter Revolution: From Good Girls to Great Women,* Bantam, 1993.
- Doumas, Christos, *The Wall-Paintings of Thera,* The Thera Foundation, 1992.
- Eliade, Mircea, *A History of Religious Ideas from the Stone Age to the Eleusinian Mysteries,* University of Chicago Press, 1978.
- Friday, Nancy, *My Mother/My Self: The Daughter's Search for Identity,* Delacorte, 1977.
- Gadon, Elinor, *The Once and Future Goddess: A Symbol for Our Time,* HarperSanFrancisco, 1989.
- Geldard, Richard G., *The Traveler's Key to Ancient Greece,* Knopf, 1989.
- Krasnow, Iris, *I Am My Mother's Daughter,* Basic Books, 2006.
- Lerner, Gerda, *The Creation of Patriarchy,* Oxford University Press, 1986.
- Marinatos, Nanno, *Art and Religion in Thera: Reconstructing a Bronze Age Society,* D. & I. Mathioulakis, 1984.
- Murdock, Maureen, *The Heroine's Journey,* Shambala, 1990.
- Neumann, Erich, *The Great Mother: Analysis of the Archetype,* Princeton University Press, 1983.
- Preka-Alexandri, Kalliope, *Eleusis,* Ministry of Culture, Archeological Receipts Fund, 2000.
- Price, T. Douglas and Anne Birgette Gebauer, eds., *Last Hunters-First Farmers,* School of American Research, 1995.
- Streep, Peg, *Sanctuaries of the Goddess: The Sacred Landscapes and Objects,* Bullfinch Press, 1994.
- Walker, Barbara G., *Womens Rituals: A Sourcebook,* HarperCollins, 1990.

Marjorie Meyers Graham

Photo by Stephen Graham

"The context for this book is my 36+ years fascination with the many layers and dimensions of ancient Greek culture. The wall frescoes found in the Bronze age archeological dig at Akrotiri reveal the joyful nature-loving spirit of the pre-patriarchal goddess-worshipping Minoan period. Inspired by the grace and power of 3,500 year-old images, I imagine new combinations and interpretations. These paintings led me to create this illustrated version of the 'real' myth of Demeter and Persephone."

A graduate of the University of Texas at Austin, Marge Graham also holds an M.A. in English and American literature from Boston College. In addition, she studied design at the University of Texas, painting and drawing at the Aegean School of Fine Arts on Paros, Greece, and landscape painting with Yianni Ziogas on Samos, Greece. She taught college English humanities and women's studies for 23 years, currently teaches women's studies and watercolor painting on Chicago's North Shore and leads artists' workshops on Crete.

Marge sits on the board of the Wilmette, Illinois Arts Guild. She is also a member of the GAIA Artist Cooperative and founder of A Woman's Place, both in New Buffalo, Michigan. She lives in Northfield, Illinois with her husband Steve. Her website is www.marjoriegraham.com.

ACKNOWLEGEMENTS

With thanks for inspiration, encouragement and help to Katherine Bateman, Susan Bennett, Angela Bowman, Kathy Burnett, Mary Ann Butkovich, Randall Darden, Dave Davenport, Suzi Donnelly, Bill Doughty, Gail Eder, Ann and Mark Feldman, Christina Fiore, Kathy Flanagan, Judi Geake, Steve Graham, Ingrid Hess, Leslie Hirschfield, Jackie Hurwitz, Judy Kauchak, Ariel Marion, Cindy Meyers, Suzanne B. Meyers, Rebecca Lynn Moll, Susan Myrick, Potter Palmer, Cheryl Perlitz, deTraci Regula, Chris Spheeris, Susan Trovas, Cate Wallace and Chris Zilke.

Grateful acknowledgment is made for permission to quote, adapt, and reproduce from: *Lost Goddesses of Early Greece: A Collection of Pre-Hellenic Myths* by Charlene Spretnak (Boston: Beacon Press, 1992); Ch. Doumas, *The Wall Paintings of Thera,* Idryma Theras-Petros M. Nomikos, Athens 1992.

Grateful acknowledgement is given to Breitman Publishing Projects; Lucy's Cards, 533 N. 31st St., Milwaukee, WI 53208; and Kalliope Preka-Alexandri.

MACEDONIA
Troy
Delphi
Thebes
Eleusis
Athens
Olympia
Mycenae
Epidaurus
Delos
CYCLADES
Akrotiri
MAP OF
ANCIENT GREECE
CRETE
Knossos
Mallia
Zakro
Phaestos
Agia Triada
Gortyn